## This Little Tiger book belongs to:

_____

_____

For Holly, with lots of love from Mum xxx ~ S M

For Karen, Mike, Tom and Louie. Lifelong friends
with superhero capabilities x ~ C P

LITTLE TIGER PRESS
1 The Coda Centre,
189 Munster Road, London SW6 6AW
www.littletigerpress.com

First published in Great Britain 2012
This edition published 2012
Text copyright © Sue Mongredien 2012
Illustrations copyright © Caroline Pedler 2012
Sue Mongredien and Caroline Pedler have asserted their rights
to be identified as the author and illustrator of this work
under the Copyright, Designs and Patents Act, 1988
A CIP catalogue record for this book
is available from the British Library

ISBN 978-1-84895-311-6
LTP/1800/0512/0912
Printed in China
10 9 8 7 6 5 4 3 2

# Super-Duper Dudley!

Sue Mongredien

Caroline Pedler

LITTLE TIGER PRESS
London

Dudley Dog was the biggest show-off in the village.
"Look at me!" he shouted,
riding his bike with no paws
on the handlebars.

"Wow, Dudley," cheered
his best friend Bonzo.
"You rule!"

"Look at me!"
Dudley yelled, dangling
daringly from Granny
Goat's apple tree.
"Wow, Dudley,"
cried Bonzo.
"You rock!"

"Look at me!" Dudley bellowed, diving dramatically into the pool.

"Wow, Dudley," breathed Bonzo. "I wish I was as awesome as you."

"Sorry, Bonzo," Dudley replied. "There's only room for one megastar in this village. And that megastar is me!"

One afternoon, Dudley fixed up a fiendishly fearsome obstacle course.

He bounced...

he swung...

he leaped ...

"Hey, Bonzo.
Look at me!"
he called.

But there was no answer.
"Strange," thought Dudley.

Then he heard some music coming from Bonzo's house – music so magnificent it made his ears quiver.

A small crowd had gathered in the garden, and through the window, Dudley saw...
Bonzo!

When Bonzo finished playing,
the crowd went crazy.
   "Bonzo is simply **sensational!**"
everyone cried.

"Bonzo – sensational?" thought Dudley. "Ha! Anyone can play plinky-plonky piano music."
And he stomped off home in an enormous sulk.

"What are you doing, Dudley?" asked Bonzo, the next day.
"Something really exciting?"

"I'm busy planning an **amazing** show," Dudley replied.
**"In private!"**

"**Wow**," Bonzo gasped. "Can I help?"

"Definitely **not**," said Dudley. "We **megastars** always work alone."

"Oh," said Bonzo.

Dudley leaped into action.

Putting on the best
show ever was
hard work!

"Wait till everyone
sees what I can do,"
he said to himself.

"They will not believe their eyes!"

Soon there were posters everywhere.

"This sounds **fantastic!**" clucked Mrs Hen.

"**Can't wait,**" woofed the dogs.

"**It's going to be a quacker!**" cried Dilys Duck.

At last it was show time.

"Look at me!"

Dudley shouted.

The audience clapped.

"Look at me!"

Dudley bellowed.

The audience cheered.

Dudley looped the loop and landed in front of a **huge** piano. "Now the moment you've all been waiting for!" he boasted. But...

"Look at me!" Dudley yelled.
The audience went **bananas!**

"**Uh-oh!**" he gulped.
"This is a total disaster."

Dudley didn't know
**what** to do.
But soon he felt a
tapping on his shoulder...

"Can I help?"
whispered Bonzo.

With Bonzo and Dudley together, the show was **spectacular!**
"Hooray!" all the animals cried.
Maybe there **was** room for
**two megastars**
in the village after all!

These
Little Tiger books
are
simply
sensational!

For information regarding any of the above titles or
for our catalogue, please contact us:
Little Tiger Press, 1 The Coda Centre,
189 Munster Road, London SW6 6AW
Tel: 020 7385 6333 • Fax: 020 7385 7333
E-mail: info@littletiger.co.uk
www.littletigerpress.com

Dudley is a daredevil superstar!
His best friend Bonzo thinks he's the best!
But Bonzo has a hidden talent,
and suddenly he's getting
all the attention. Can the two
young pups share the spotlight,
and still be friends?

This book is perfect
for any budding
superstar!

Little Tiger Press

ISBN 978-1-84895-311-6

£5.99

9 781848 953116

www.littletigerpress.com